I LOVE MY NOSE!

-By Sherry Selley -

Illustrated by Mary Navarro

ISBN : 978-0-9959302-0-9
www.aroundtheblockpublishing.com
AroundTheBlockPublishing@gmail.com

I LOVE MY NOSE!

— DEACON —

DeDicatioN

to my husband and 3 sons.
THANK YOU for always supporting my crazy
projects
and for just letting me, be ME!

I hope that you ALWAYS follow the voice in your
head that says: "YES, I can DO IT"!

"USE THIS BOOK TO GET THEM LISTENING, GET THEM TALKING, AND TO PLANT THE SEEDS FOR A LIFE DRIVEN BY SELF-LOVE."

— SHERRY SELLEY —

-AUTHOR SHERRY SELLEY, AGE 3-

I love My Nose

MY NAME IS MAGGIE!

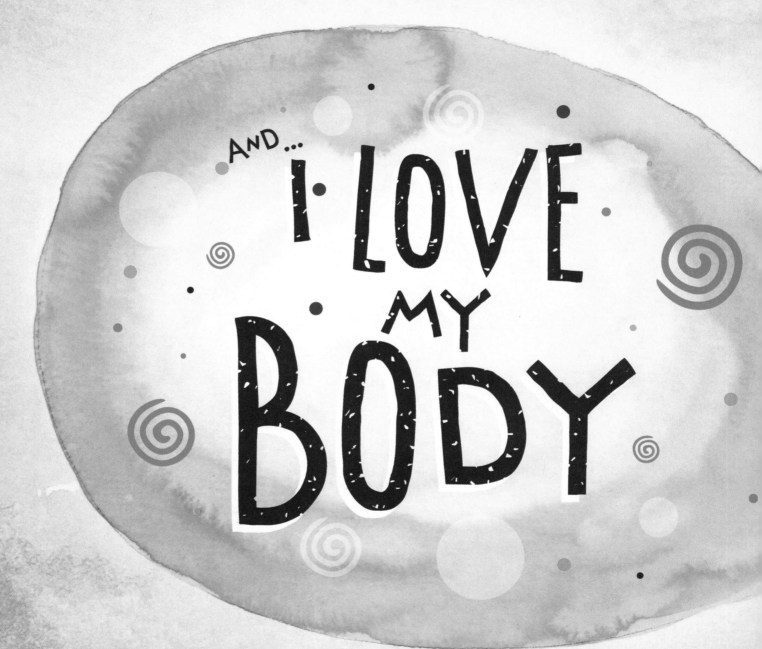

AND... I LOVE MY BODY

MY BODY IS CRAZY SPECIAL!

AND UNIQUE IN ITS OWN WAY

By Sherry Selley 13

WANNA KNOW WHAT I LOVE ABOUT IT?

'CAUSE I'LL TELL YA!

I LOVE MY HAIR

I love my hair because it's beautiful! My hair is big and fluffy and keeps my head warm!

WHAT DO YOU LOVE ABOUT YOUR HAIR?

I LOVE MY EYES

My eyes are so pretty! I love my eyes
because they help me see my bug collection

WHAT DO YOU LOVE ABOUT YOUR EYES?

I LOVE MY ARMS

I love my arms because they are strong!
My arms help me climb on the monkey bars!

SO TELL ME...
WHAT DO YOU
LOVE ABOUT
YOUR ARMS?

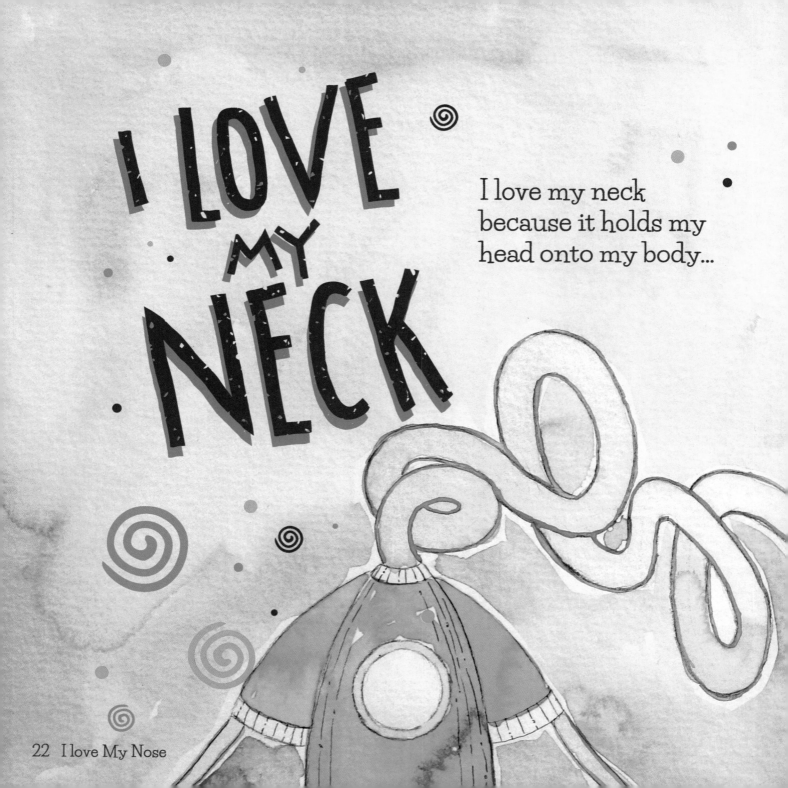

I LOVE MY NECK

I love my neck because it holds my head onto my body...

By Sherry Selley 23

AND THAT IS CRAZY IMPORTANT

WELL...
DO YA?

MY FAVORITE
BODY PART IS...

MY
NOSE!

By Sherry Selley 29

I LOVE MY NOSE!

I love it because it helps me to smell my
baba's freshly baked cinnamon rolls!
THEY SMELL SOOOOO GOOD!!

Yep! I sure do LOVE

ALL THE PARTS OF
MY BODY

Every night when i have a bubble bath I WASH and THANK each part of my body for what it does for me!

THANK YOU HANDS!
AND THANK YOU FEET!

My friends and I **all** think...

THAT OUR BODIES ARE JUST PERFECT IN EVERY WAY

And we think that
YOURS IS TOO!

SO, TELL ME... WHAT DO YOU LOVE ABOUT YOUR BODY?

THE END

Made in the USA
Middletown, DE
20 September 2022

10772402R00024